Tootle and Katy Caboose
A Special Treasure

By Gina Ingoglia
Illustrated by Isidre Mones

A GOLDEN BOOK • NEW YORK
Western Publishing Company, Inc., Racine, Wisconsin 53404

There is a magical place called Little Golden Book Land, filled with wonderful things to see and do. Every day is a special day, just waiting to be discovered.

The bears were giving a springtime party in Cavetown.

"We're going to have a treasure hunt," said Baby Brown Bear's father. "Look all around. Find something you think is very special and bring it back. Then we'll all share our treasures."

The big bear blew his whistle, and the hunt began.

"This is awful," said Katy Caboose. "What kind of special treasure is going to be in the middle of a train track?"

"I don't know," said Tootle. "But, remember, we can never go off the track."

"I know," said Katy Caboose with a sigh.

"Let's look anyway. Something may turn up," said Tootle, and off they went.

Poky Little Puppy knew right away what his treasure was going to be. He had buried a big bone a few weeks ago in the playground and all he had to do was dig it up.

"Bones are special," he thought. "They keep your teeth clean and healthy. Best of all, they taste good."

He took off for the playground in a flash.

Saggy Baggy Elephant quickly found his treasure. It was right behind Baby Brown Bear's house in Cavetown.

"I can't believe it," he said. "This is the most beautiful rock I've ever seen. It looks all wrinkly—just like me!"

The little elephant pushed the big rock with his trunk.

"This rock is extra-special. It's not only the best-looking treasure, it's the heaviest."

Tootle stared hard at the winding train track.

"Any luck?" asked Katy Caboose.

"No," said Tootle. "Do you see anything?"

"Not a thing," said Katy Caboose. "We might as well head back."

"Let's not give up just yet," said Tootle as they chugged on.

Scuffy the tugboat bobbed down a little stream.
"Not a single treasure in sight," he thought.

Suddenly a tiny frog hopped right onto Scuffy's
deck.

"Hi," said Scuffy. "I'm on a treasure hunt. I have
to find something special."

"That's nice," said the frog.

"Would you like to be my treasure?" asked
Scuffy. "You're special. You can hop and you're
green."

"Okay," said the frog. "I've never been a treasure
before."

Tootle and Katy Caboose had traveled all over
Little Golden Book Land and still hadn't found
any special treasures.

"Nothing is pretty or shiny or different on the
train tracks," moaned Katy Caboose.

"Maybe *we* aren't even special," said Tootle.
"We can't ever leave the train tracks and go off
with everyone else."

"Maybe you're right," agreed Katy Caboose.
The two sadly headed back to Cavetown.

Shy Little Kitten decided to look for her treasure in the daisy patch.

She sniffed and searched and searched and sniffed. Once she even sneezed. And then she stumbled upon a four-leaf clover.

"This is a special treasure," she thought. "Four-leaf clovers are very lucky." Shy Little Kitten picked it and then padded back to the party.

Baby Brown Bear climbed a tree and looked around.

He didn't have to look far. Right next to him was a large beehive. "A treasure!" cried Baby Brown Bear. "Hives are special. They have honey in them."

Baby Brown Bear looked closely at the hive. "Good," he said. "There are no bees inside."

He climbed down the tree very carefully. He didn't want to drop his treasure.

Tootle and Katy Caboose were almost back in Cavetown when Tootle stopped short.

"Listen," he said. "I think I hear someone crying. It sounds like it's coming from that tunnel up ahead."

The little engine switched on his bright headlight. Then he and Katy Caboose advanced into the dark opening.

"Look!" said Tootle. "It's one of the baby rabbits."

The tiny animal stopped crying when he saw his friends.

"I'm so happy to see you," he said. "I wasn't supposed to go off by myself, but I did. Then I got lost."

"It's lucky we found you," said Tootle. "Hop aboard. We'll take you back to the party."

Everyone cheered when Tootle and Katy Caboose
returned to Cavetown with the missing rabbit.

"You two found a very special treasure," said Baby
Brown Bear's father.

"But we would always help anyone that was lost
or needed a ride," said Tootle.

"That's what makes you both so special," said the
big bear. "Anything is special when you care about
it," he explained. "And we all care about you two
very much."